# BIG BAD BUNNY

Alan Durant ★ illustrated by Guy Parker-Rees

Dutton Children's Books ★ New York

For Josie, whose idea this was
A.D.
To Bun in the oven and Bun's mum
G.P.R.

Text copyright © 2000 by Alan Durant
Illustrations copyright © 2000 by Guy Parker-Rees
All rights reserved.

CIP Data is available.

Published in the United States 2001 by Dutton Children's Books,
a division of Penguin Putnam Books for Young Readers
345 Hudson Street, New York, New York 10014
www.penguinputnam.com

Originally published in Great Britain 2000 by Orchard Books, London
Printed in Hong Kong    First American Edition
ISBN 0-525-46667-3
2  4  6  8  10  9  7  5  3  1

**H**ere comes Big Bad Bunny.

He's coming to get your money!

Down the road goes
Big Bad Bunny.
He sees a little chick.

"Little Chick, give me your money!"
cries Big Bad Bunny.

But Little Chick hasn't got any money.
All she has is a little bit of corn.
"I'll take that!" cries Big Bad Bunny.
Then off he goes to get some money.

Down the road goes Big Bad Bunny.
He sees a little squirrel.
"Little Squirrel, give me your money!"
cries Big Bad Bunny.

But Little Squirrel hasn't got any money.
All he has is one little nut.

"I'll take that!" cries Big Bad Bunny.
Then off he goes to get some money.

Down the road goes Big Bad Bunny.
He sees a little goat.

"Little Goat, give me your money!"
cries Big Bad Bunny.

But Little Goat hasn't got any money.
All he has is a little bit of milk.

"I'll take that!" cries Big Bad Bunny.
Then off he goes to get some money.

FROM BIG BAD BUNNY?

Into town goes Big Bad Bunny.

He *wants* to get some money.

At the counter is Wise Old Bunny.
"Give me your money!" cries Big Bad Bunny.
"I want it all. I want it now!"

"*All* my money?" says Wise Old Bunny.
"*All* your money!" cries You Know Who.
"Well, OK," sighs Wise Old Bunny.
"Hold out your hands."

"There's one bag of money," says Wise Old Bunny,
"two, three, four, five, six, seven, eight…"

Big Bad Bunny's
legs disappear.

Big Bad Bunny's
hands disappear.

Big Bad Bunny's
neck disappears.

"Yikes!" cries Big Bad Bunny.
Big Bad Bunny's head disappears!
All that is left of Big Bad Bunny
are the tips of his ears—and the bags of money.

"Let me out!" shouts Big Bad Bunny.
"If you want to get out," says Wise Old Bunny,
"you must give back all you took and say you're sorry.
And promise never again to take our money."

"OK, I promise," squeaks Big Bad Bunny.

So back up the road
goes Big Bad Bunny.
He gives back
the milk to
Little Goat.

"Sorry, Little Goat,"
says Big Bad Bunny.

He gives back
the nut to
Little Squirrel.
"Sorry, Little Squirrel,"
says Big Bad Bunny.

He gives back the corn
to Little Chick.

"Sorry, Little Chick,"
says Big Bad Bunny.

Big Bad Bunny feels sorry and sad.
He's had enough of being bad.

"How can I show them I want to be nice?
I'll bake them a pie with sugar and spice!"

Back in town...
Everyone is safe now—so is their money.
But things are QUIET with no Big Bad Bunny.

The ribbon on the cake reads: To all my friends

"But, hey, what's this?"
says Wise Old Bunny.

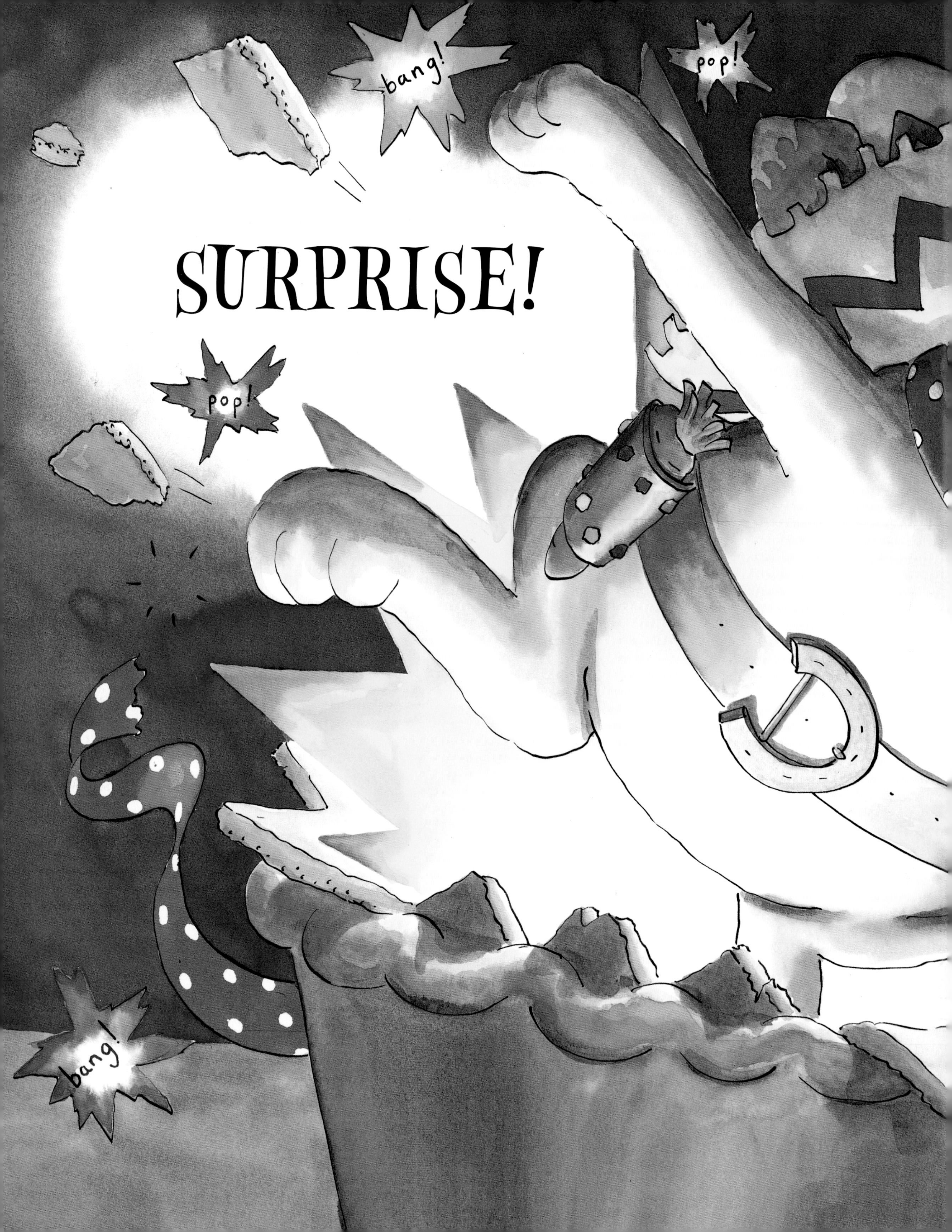


SURPRISE!

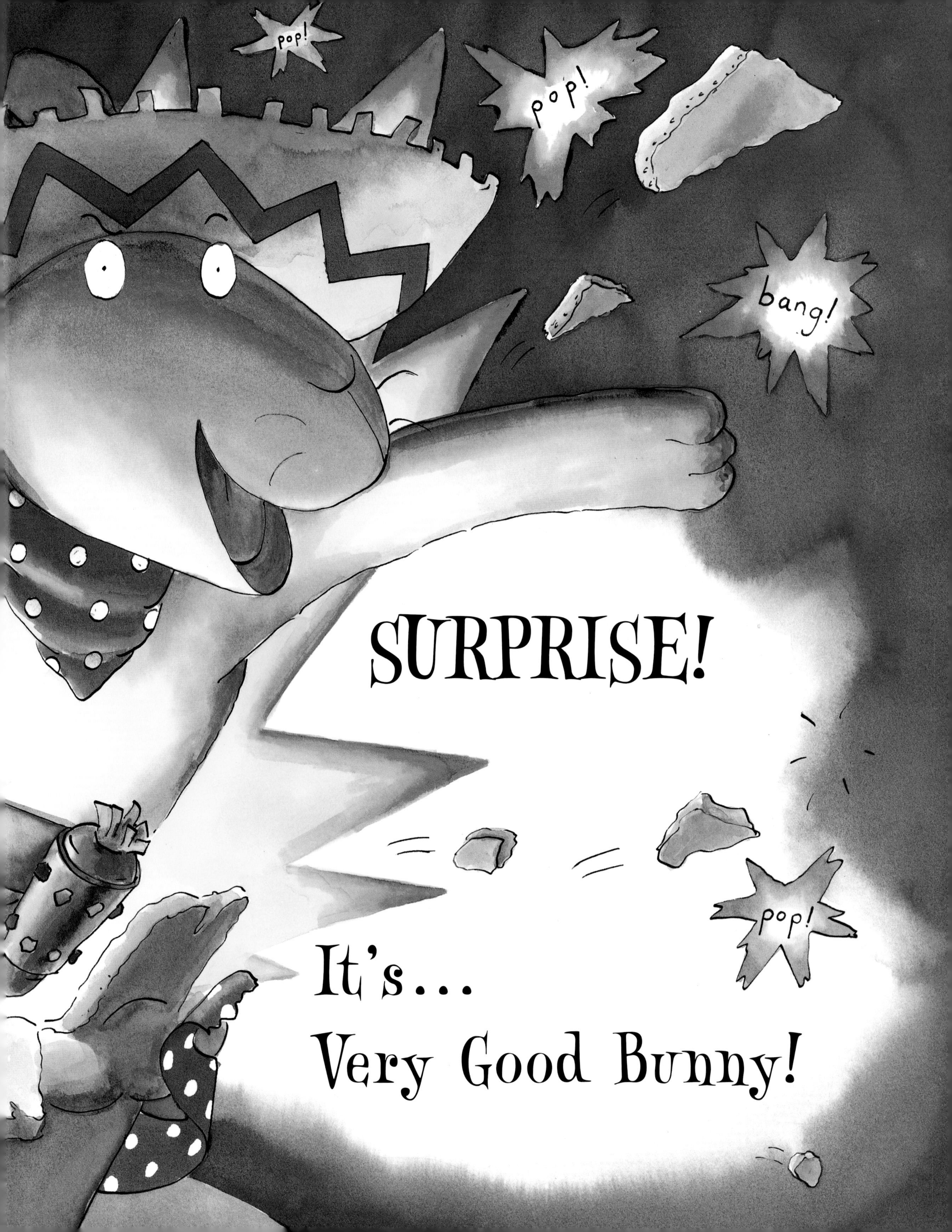


SURPRISE!

It's...
Very Good Bunny!

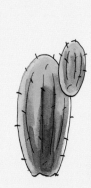